Visit us on the Web!
HairandNowGlobal.com • Facebook.com/HairandNowGlobal
Twitter.com/HairandNowGloba • Instagram.com/HairandNowGlobal
Pinterest.com/HairandNowGlobal • @HairandNowGlobal

Copyright © 2019 by HairandNowGlobal
All rights reserved.

Mom, where is your hair? — First Edition.
Alicia Gleeson-Cherneski, Author
Brianna Gleeson, Illustrator
Summary: Illustrations and simple, rhyming text reveal a curious child's search for their mother's hair.

No part of this publication may be reproduced, stored in a retrieval system, or transmitted in any form, or by any means, electronic, mechanical, photocopying, recording, or otherwise, without written permission of the publisher. For information regarding permission, write to HairandNowGlobal.com. The text in this book is DK Mama Bear.

ISBN 978-0-473-48271-8 (Softcover) • ISBN 978-0-473-48272-5 (epub) • ISBN 978-0-473-48273-2 (hardcover)
ISBN 978-0-473-48274-9 (kindle) • ISBN 978-0-473-48275-6 (iBook)

Mom, Where is Your Hair?

Written by Alicia Gleeson-Cherneski   Illustrated by Brianna Gleeson

Mom, where is your hair? I will find it, I will look everywhere!

I jumped aboard a ship,
and sailed across the world with captain Flip.
We sailed the seven seas, and asked everyone "Please?"
While sailing around the islands, some pirates came and stole our diamonds.
For sure they must've stolen your hair. So we followed them to a fair.

2

Inside their tent, we hunted everywhere. Instead, we got quite a scare.
The walls were lined with caged magical things.
We ran to free them from their strings.
Your hair was nowhere in sight, but we got quite a fright.
We were surrounded by pirates ready to fight.
But a wonderful and caring creature, who was a gnome,
saved us and brought us home.

Mom, I looked here, there, and everywhere,
but I can't find your hair, anywhere!

Mom, where is your hair? I will find it, I will look everywhere!

I spoke to the grasshoppers and dragonflies.
They make quite good spies.
They told me to speak to the fairies, the ones that live near the berries.
I danced all about, until the fairies came out.
They took my hand, and flew me to their fairyland.

I searched high, I searched low, I searched as far as my eye could go.
The fairies checked every flower, mushroom, and lake.
But there was no sign of your hair to take.
I wondered and I pondered where it could be!
When a superstar fairy named Zoey, sat next to me.
We laughed, played, and joked until it was late,
then she brought me home through the fairy gate.

Mom, I looked here, there, and everywhere,
but I can't find your hair, anywhere!

Mom, where is your hair? I will find it, I will look everywhere!

Animals have so much hair. Perhaps they have yours spare?
Sam the happy elephant would not forget, so off to animal kingdom I set.
I found Sam and asked if he knew.
He said he did not, "But do you need a hairdo?"

Giji the giraffe told me to climb aboard.
Perhaps I would find your hair in a spot unexplored.

In the distance I saw a mane,
but when I was near, I saw it was a lion named Zane.

The monkeys swung in the treetops in search of your hair,
and the hippos searched in the pond, so did the bear.

I'm sorry Mom, we couldn't find it anywhere, so home I come.

Mom, I looked here, there, and everywhere,
but I can't find your hair, anywhere!

12

Mom, where is your hair? I will find it, I will look everywhere!

Your hair always falls out when wet.
It must be at the bottom of the sea, I bet!

I jumped in a submarine to check.
While drifting below I came across a wreck.

There were pearls, purses, and treasure galore,
tangled with a sunken ship on the sea floor.

14

I drifted in through a swirl of colourful hair. There were mermaids everywhere!
They swayed and danced from side to side,
as I bobbed along in my ride.

An amazing mermaid asked me what's wrong. I said that your hair was gone.
With a click of her fingers, her hair disappeared.
"You are beautiful no matter what" she said.
And with that, I drifted home to bed.

Mom, I looked here, there, and everywhere,
but I can't find your hair, anywhere!

Mom, where is your hair? I will find it, I will look everywhere!

Perhaps if I found a lucky leprechaun to grant my wish,
I could get you new hair and a pet fish!
Off I went in search of a magical rainbow,
and came across one with a golden glow.

Violet, indigo, blue, that was my first clue.
Red, orange, yellow, green, the leprechaun I have finally seen.
He was quick and moved in a flash,
I tried to grab him, but he would dash.
No matter what I did, he could not be landed,
home I came, empty-handed.

19

Mom, I looked here, there, and everywhere,
but I can't find your hair, anywhere!

Mom, where is your hair?

My hair is gone, I don't know for how long.
It has left my head, I'm bald instead.
I'm healthy and well, so please don't dwell.
I may look different and people may stare,
but I am still the same, and I am still here.

Mom, you don't have hair, but I don't care.
You are wonderful and caring the way you are,
you are my superstar.
You make me so happy, I love you a lot,
you are beautiful no matter what.
I am lucky to have you. You are the best.
Let's not worry about the rest!

The End

Do you have friends who have lost their hair?
Show them your support, color this in, and share.

share @HairandNowGlobal

Has someone you love lost their hair?
Color this in and share.

share @HairandNowGlobal

About the Author

Alicia was born with alopecia. Alopecia is defined as a partial or complete absence of hair from areas of the body where it would normally grow, including the scalp! For Alicia's entire life, she has had very little hair on her head, eyebrows, and eyelashes.

Losing your hair is not easy. Alicia knows that first hand, after initially letting hair loss impact her self-esteem and confidence. Now, Alicia has set out on a global adventure to find hair loss solutions and help others with hair loss or hair imperfections along the way. One of the biggest things Alicia has learned is that hair loss impacts every nationality, in every single country in the World, and that no one needs to go through it alone.

Increasing awareness and talking about hair loss is a great way to change perceptions and increase society's acceptance of everyone's hair. You can help! By talking about hair loss and spreading the word, you may help make at least one person's hair loss that much easier, helping their self-esteem and confidence.

Alicia has many more adventurous stories about hair loss, so stay tuned or follow along on the web!

HairandNowGlobal.com • Facebook.com/HairandNowGlobal
Twitter.com/HairandNowGloba • Instagram.com/HairandNowGlobal
@HairandNowGlobal

Made in the USA
Coppell, TX
11 July 2023

19029682R00019